W9-BWP-606

JACK AND THE WILD LIFE

Also by Lisa Doan

The Berenson Schemes #1:
Jack the Castaway

PAR AVION
INDIA

JACK AND THE WILD LIFE

By Lisa Doan

illustrations by Ivica Stevanovic

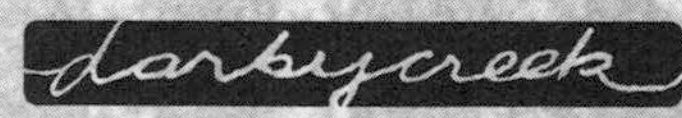

MINNEAPOLIS

Darby Creek
A division of Lerner Publishing Group, Inc.
241 First Avenue North
Minneapolis, MN 55401 USA

For reading levels and more information, look up this title at www.lernerbooks.com.

Cover and interior images © iStockphoto.com/subjug (mail envelope); © Christian Mueringer/Dreamstime.com (vintage postage stamp); © iStockphoto.com/blondiegirl (postage meter); © ilolab/Shutterstock.com (wood background); © Picsfive/Shutterstock.com (note paper); © CWB/Shutterstock.com (passport stamps); © Tsyhun/Shutterstock.com (canvas passport background).

Main body text set in Janson Text LT Std 12/17.5.
Typeface provided by Linotype AG.

Library of Congress Cataloging-in-Publication Data

Doan, Lisa.
Jack and the wild life / by Lisa Doan ; illustrated by Ivica Stevanovic.
pages cm. — (The Berenson schemes ; #2)
Summary: Jack's parents have decided to guide safaris in Africa, much to Jack's chagrin, and none of their previous schemes have worked.
ISBN 978–1–4677–1077–0 (trade hard cover : alk. paper)
ISBN 978–1–4677–4643–4 (eBook)
[1. Adventure and adventurers—Fiction. 2. Safaris—Fiction. 3. Parents—Fiction. 4. Eccentrics and eccentricities—Fiction. 5. Africa—Fiction. 6. Humorous stories.] I. Title.
PZ7.D6485Jab 2014
[Fic]—dc23 2013023167

Manufactured in the United States of America
1 – SB – 7/15/14

VIA AIR MAIL

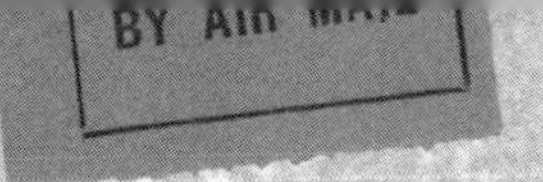

For Brandon and Holly Robison,
my nephew and niece, who have
starred in some of my earlier works,
including such classics as *A Very
Zombie Christmas*

Special thanks to April Murray for
her insightful review to ensure a
respectful portrayal of the
Maasai people

The Berenson Family Decision-Making Rules

If you are Jack, don't assume the worst will happen. Imagine what Richard and Claire would do and then take out the life-threatening parts.

If you are Richard and Claire, don't assume everything will be fine. Try to imagine what Jack would do. If Jack would never do what you're thinking about doing, that is a warning sign!

If we all follow the rules, we will probably survive.

In which Jack learns of another scheme

Jack's parents hovered over the sofa, shoving clothes into duffel bags. Jack tiptoed across the living room. Standing behind them, he whispered, "What are you doing? Running away?"

Richard and Claire Berenson whirled to face Jack. They looked as if they had been caught robbing a bank.

"You *are* running away!" Jack said. "Without me?" Jack thought his family had finally settled into a comfortable routine. They were back in his old neighborhood in Pennsylvania, with the Berenson Family Rules hung on the refrigerator.

"Jack," his dad said, "there you are. Right there behind us."

"Don't be a goose, Jack," his mom said. "Of course we're not running away. If we ever go on the run, you'll be the first thing we pack. We're just—"

"Organizing," his dad said.

"Organizing?" Jack said. That wasn't likely. "Tell me what's going on."

"Oh, we did try to tell you," his mom said.

"Spelled it out every which way," his dad added.

"Remember, Jack," his mom said, "when we went to the Renaissance Fair for dinner? Right through the whole jousting tournament, your dad and I observed that life is an adventure. Don't you adore airports, we asked, and aren't elephants amazing, and isn't camping divine?"

Jack did remember that. He had told the medieval serving wench not to give them any more mead. "What were you trying to tell me?"

His mom blurted out, "We're going to Africa!"

CHAPTER 2

In which Richard and Claire Berenson reveal new career developments

"What do you mean, we're going to Africa?" Jack asked.

"Hold on, Son," his dad said, "you haven't even heard the most thrilling part. Your mum and I have invented a brand-new kind of tourism."

"Oh, no," Jack muttered.

"Now, just hear us out," his dad said. "This time, we've hit upon a surefire moneymaking opportunity."

"This one can't lose," his mom said.

"Thousands of people travel to Kenya each year," his dad said. "Every one of them becomes fascinated by the noble and revered Maasai people. But do these travelers come away with any true understanding of the Maasai way of life? No! They just think they did because they bought a necklace and took a photo."

"But three years ago, we employed a Maasai elder as a safari guide," his mom said. "We even stayed overnight with his family before we flew home. Meticiki was so fond of us, there were tears in his eyes when we said good-bye. Even his children were crying."

"Kenya had a place in our hearts forever," his dad said. "So when we found ourselves trying out the old nine-to-five grind this summer, I said to your mum, I bet Meticiki doesn't work nine to five."

"And I said, too bad *we* weren't born Maasai elders," his mom said.

"Then it hit me like a lightning bolt," Jack's dad said. "Let's build a camp where tourists can live like a real Maasai tribe!"

Jack's mom hooked her thumb at his dad. "That's where you get your smarts from, Jack. That man right there."

His dad blushed. "I'm a bit surprised nobody thought of it before now."

"It's brilliant," his mom said. "In fact, there are layers of brilliance to it. For example, we won't have to spend millions of dollars building a luxury safari lodge with a swimming pool. Which is splendid, since we don't have millions of dollars."

"Yet," his dad said.

Jack wondered if the room was actually spinning or if his brain just couldn't compute what he had heard. He gripped the nearest arm of the sofa.

"You see, Son," his dad said, "the Maasai live in the kind of housing we can construct ourselves. We'll start by building an *enkang* of acacia thorns."

"An *enkang* is a fence to keep out lions," his mom said.

"Lions!" Jack cried.

"Indeed. Nobody wants a lion hanging about the place," his dad said. "Once we have the *enkang* up, we build the *inkajijik*."

"That's the house," his mom said.

"Here's another layer of brilliance," his dad said. "We won't have to buy building materials. Not even a nail. It's all right there for us in the great outdoors. Mud, sticks, and grass, free to anybody that comes along."

"Except for the cow dung to make it all stick together," his mom said. "But we'll buy a cow, and then all we have to do is wait."

"And thanks to you, Son, we'll be planning ahead for disasters. If the cow dung doesn't hold up, we'll reinforce the whole thing with duct tape."

Jack blinked. How was duct-taping a house together supposed to be his idea?

"The catering won't cost us either," his dad continued. "The Maasai don't wander around Walmart, shopping for sales on Cocoa Puffs; they live off the land. The guests can milk the cow, and we'll leave them a couple of spears for hunting. They'll be out on their own, having the adventure of a lifetime."

"They'll cook whatever they hunt over a campfire," his mom said, "so we won't have to buy a stove."

"We won't even need electricity."

"Or plumbing."

"You see what we mean by layers of brilliance?" his dad asked.

"So, you want people to fly all the way to Africa and pay you to let them stay in a hut you built out of cow dung and duct tape. Then, if the roof doesn't crash down on their heads, they can run around with a spear trying to kill a wild animal for dinner? That is the worst idea I've ever heard."

"You always say that," his mom said. "But it's not actually possible for all of our ideas to be *the* worst idea. Jack, you're not seeing the genius of it. People will pay for the unique experience. They can stay in a nice hotel any day, but living like a real Maasai tribe? Now that's a once-in-a-lifetime adventure!"

Jack did not point out that all the people his parents had treated to a once-in-a-lifetime adventure were still trying to forget it. "They'll sue you. Something will go horribly wrong, and they'll sue you."

"Not this time, Son," his dad said. "We're going at this like professional businesspeople.

We even printed out a contract. 'The Berenson Camp Company is not liable for any inconvenience, including yellow fever, elephant stampedes, lightning strikes, snakebites, flash floods, and anything else that results in illness and injury up to and including death.'"

"We found a sample contract on the internet and just switched it up a bit," his mom said. "Your dad came up with the 'and anything else' part to really cover all the bases. How's that for planning?"

"Nobody will sign something like that!" Jack said.

"Listen, luv," his mom said, "we've worked at the Sub Stop for the entire summer, slapping together sandwiches and pita pockets. Us! The Berensons! We've been reduced to pita pockets, when we should be millionaires by now. And after all that hard work, Mr. Kringlenuffer said . . . " His mom paused, then mumbled, "Actually, I blocked out what he said."

"His exact words were," his dad said, "'that's it, I've had it, get out, and no, I will not give you references.'"

Jack's mom patted his dad's arm. "You couldn't have known how hot those peppers were."

His dad nodded. "It turns out Mrs. Kramer does not care for habanero. Though 'even my eyes are on fire' was a *bit* dramatic."

"You lost your jobs," Jack said. "Again! Both of you, at the same time?"

"It's not so much a loss as it is a sign," his mom said. "When you put it together with the eviction notice—"

"We're getting evicted!?"

"Apparently," his dad muttered, "the landlord never did get over the fireworks incident. *Somebody* doesn't care to celebrate this great country's independence."

"You burned down the garage," Jack said. "He probably doesn't think a two-alarm fire counts as a celebration."

Jack's breathing had become fast and shallow. He ran to the kitchen, fished a paper lunch bag out of a drawer, and breathed into it.

"Now, Jack, there's no reason to hyperventilate," his mom said, trailing after him.

"Take deep breaths and remember the family rules. We swear this trip will be different."

His dad followed and said, "Your mom and I have made remarkable strides in planning and organization."

Jack thought "remarkable strides" was a little optimistic. Or a lot optimistic.

"And," his mom said, "you've been so good about depositing our paychecks and hiding the debit card that we actually have savings. Now we can parlay them into a real fortune."

"That's right," his dad said. "All the great financial minds parlay. It's the only way to get ahead in this world. Did Warren Buffet ever work at the Sub Stop? No, he was too busy parlaying."

"I don't know anything about Warren Buffet or parlaying, but the last thing we should do is go to a foreign country," Jack said. "After . . . you know."

His mom stared at the linoleum; his dad played with the string to the ceiling fan. "Jack," his dad said, "no need to dwell on the past. The only thing to remember about the past is that it is now over. Your mom and I have put those kinds of mishaps behind us. These days, we're thinking ahead. Thinking, thinking, thinking."

"We're practically running a think tank around here," his mom said.

"Number one: losing your son in the ocean is more than a 'mishap,'" Jack said. "Number two: we were deported. It's stamped right in our passports! And number three: I had to phone Ms. Seldie and ask if she was enjoying her time with our parrot, since we weren't coming back. Thank goodness she likes birds."

"Quite the mix-up," his mom said. "As if we would ever knowingly insult a culture's heritage."

Jack said, "I told you to put that stone carving back. I told you the taxi driver was calling the police."

"We thought you were kidding," his dad said. "What kind of person calls the police over a rock?"

"Anyway, it all worked out for the best," his mom said. "You've spent the whole summer here with that cute girlfriend."

Jack felt the familiar burn on his face. Every time somebody mentioned Diana, it sent some kind of signal to his blood, which then fired up, barreled down his veins, and exploded onto his cheeks. He had privately named it "the race to the face."

"She's not my girlfriend!" Jack said, in a voice that came out higher than he had planned.

Jack wasn't actually sure if Diana was his girlfriend or not. He spent a lot of time examining the clues. Some seemed to say yes, while others seemed to say no. He had thought about asking her, but every time he tried to imagine the conversation, he had the urge to step into a dark closet and quietly close the door behind him. So far, he had just waited for the clues to pile up on one side or the other.

He was still analyzing the clue from the annual county fair. He, Diana, and Zack had gone to the arcade. Jack had been determined to win her a stuffed animal, and he'd practiced with a dartboard for weeks. He figured he could casually hand her the biggest prize they had and say, "I'm a guy. Not into stuffed animals. Here, you can have it." But no, *she* had won a stuffed animal and given it to *him*.

He now possessed a small brown monkey with Velcro paws that Diana had named Mack. Jack had been forced to carry the thing all over the fair. Zack had helpfully pointed out "Jack's special friend" to every single person from school that they had run into.

Near the end of the night, Diana had suggested they get photos. She had squeezed into the booth next to him and insisted he hold Mack on his lap like a human baby. What did that mean?

Jack's dad poked him in the ribs and said, "What a summer, eh? You, your girlfriend, and your wingman Zack tearing up the town like a pack of wild rebels."

"You're getting off the subject," Jack said. "You don't know anything about Maasai tribes or building camps or guiding tourists in Africa."

"Oh, we know about tour guiding in Africa," his mom said. "Remember, we actually owned a safari business."

"You told me you lost two old people in the

wilderness. Didn't you get deported for that? Doesn't that mean you can't ever go back?"

"We left Kenya under our own steam," his mom said. "We only had to swear never to lead another safari and or go within fifty feet of that Grady couple. And we didn't lose them. We accidentally left them behind at Lake Nakuru."

"There was no mention of being banned from building a Maasai camp. None whatsoever."

"Come now, luv," his mom said, "We're even hiring a technical consultant to advise us. The idea seemed like such an unnecessary bother, we were sure we were on the right track."

Jack thought that did sound more like the kind of thing he would do. He wondered what the catch was.

"That's right, Son. We've already sent a letter to Meticiki," his dad said. "Our old friend can fill in the blanks on all things Maasai. Then we'll parlay into our fortune, and you'll be back in time for Christmas."

"Jack, I know what's really on your mind," his mom said. "But we have finally got it through our heads how obsessed you are about your education. I've ordered a book that covers all of seventh grade. By the time you get back, you'll be ahead of your schoolmates."

"And we'll even give you homework," his dad added, "if you absolutely insist on it."

Jack had spent the summer catching up on what he had missed while living on an uninhabited island in the Caribbean. He still wondered how he would explain that episode of his life in his Harvard application essay.

"But maybe it would be better if I stayed here," he said. "I could stay with Zack." Jack felt bad saying it. His parents had been away most of his life, and they were all just getting to know each other. Still, a stay at Zack's did seem like the safer option. His parents had tried to be more careful and plan ahead, but caution wasn't a skill that came naturally to them. If they got a safety report card, it would probably be a D with an enthusiastic note from the teacher about how they'd earned an A for effort.

His dad flushed. "We swore we'd never leave you behind again. From here on in, the Berensons stick together."

"Like the Three Musketeers," his mom said.

"Like a knife, fork, and spoon," his dad said.

"Like Snap, Crackle, and Pop."

"Like Bonnie, Clyde, and . . . their son," his dad said.

"Bonnie and Clyde were criminals," Jack said.

"Then," his mom said, "like the three blind mice."

That one was probably closer to the truth.

"We promise this time will be different," his mom said. "We'll be so cautious, we'll bore ourselves. We'll plan until we fall into a planning coma. We'll tattoo the family rules on our foreheads."

"We won't even pick a restaurant at the spur of the moment," his dad added. "We will be methodical."

"Me-thod-i-cal," his mom said.

Jack's shoulders slumped. "You already bought three plane tickets, didn't you?"

"Yes, we did," his dad said.

• • •

Jack had spent two hours wandering up and down Diana's street, trying to look as though he was on his way to the library, before he finally ran into her.

"Hey," Jack said.

"Hey," Diana answered.

"So I'm going on a trip. I'll be back at Christmas."

"Oh. Where?"

"Kenya."

"I've never been there."

"No?"

"No."

There was a long pause. The kind of pause Jack dreaded.

"You know what you could do?" Diana said.

"What?" Jack asked, thinking he sounded a little desperate.

"You could bring Mack and take photos of him. You know, like people do with lawn gnomes."

"They take lawn gnomes?"

"Yeah. It's called gnoming," she said.

"Oh. Gnoming."

"Then you could send me postcards about where you took him."

That night, in his room, Jack stared at the photo Diana had given him from their time in the photo booth. She was smiling and looking great. Jack looked like he was staring at a ghost. He could only imagine his expression in the two pictures she had kept. Now, he had agreed to take the monkey gnoming and to send Diana postcards. What did that mean?

In which Jack learns what Meticiki has agreed to, which is nothing

The plane dropped beneath the clouds, descending toward Jomo Kenyatta Airport.

"Is this Meticiki person meeting us at the gate?" Jack said.

"That would be a convenient surprise," his dad said.

"Where is he, then?"

"No worries, Son, we'll find him," his dad said.

"Find him?" Jack asked. "But you wrote to him. Didn't you get a letter back?"

His mom patted his arm. "You know how the post is."

"A day late and a dollar short," his dad said with a knowing nod. "That's the Post Office for you."

"So you never heard back from him?" Jack said. "What if he says no? How are we going to find him to ask? Do you have his phone number?"

Jack's mom and dad looked hopefully at each other, like the other person should field the question.

"You probably don't even know where he lives!" Jack said.

"Not true, Jack," his dad said. "Meticiki lives in the Rift Valley."

"We'll just rent a car, and off we go," his mom said. "Simplest thing in the world. And, Jack, the idea that anybody would turn down this opportunity—can you even imagine?"

Jack could imagine.

• • •

Richard and Claire Berenson spent forty-five minutes explaining to the immigration official the series of mix-ups that had led to their deportation from six other countries. The man stamped their passports and muttered, "That's a lot of mix-ups."

The taxi barreled down the Mombasa Road toward downtown Nairobi. The cracked-open windows let in a rush of crisp air. Jack gripped the door handle. If there were any speed limits, the driver didn't care what they were.

"Jack," his mom said, "we've really embraced your whole notion of planning ahead. You'll be impressed with some of the things we packed. Not like the last time, when we had to go out and buy toothbrushes."

"That's right, Son. If it hadn't been for your sage and practical influence, your mom and I would never have thought to bring . . . should we tell him?"

"Let's do," his mom said.

His dad wrestled with his overstuffed carry-on pack.

"Look," his mom said, "walkie-talkies!"

Jack stared at the yellow walkie-talkies encased in plastic. "Why wouldn't we just use our cell phones?"

"Oh, they won't work. Not where we're going."

His mom ripped open the package and handed his dad one of the receivers. She held the other one up to her mouth and said, "Mama bird calling papa bird. Do you read me, papa bird?"

"Roger that, mama bird. Papa bird is over and out," his dad answered.

"Jack, you can be—"

"I'm not being baby bird," Jack said. "But I'm impressed. If we run into trouble, we can call for help. That's really good planning. Do the police in Kenya have a special number or code to use in an emergency?"

His dad squinted at the tiny pamphlet that had come with the walkie-talkies. "Ah. I see. These devices only talk to each other."

Jack suppressed a sigh. "What's the range?"

"One hundred yards."

"But we could just yell to each other from that distance," Jack pointed out.

Jack's mom slumped in her seat. "Richard, remember when we saw them and thought,

'Now here's a brilliant parenting moment? Jack wants us to think ahead, and a person can't think further ahead than this.'"

"Like it was yesterday," his dad said. "We were certain we were on the right track. How did we get it so wrong?"

"My sister Julia used to say we were the worst parents in the world," Jack's mom said. "We always thought she was barmy on the subject, but do you suppose she was on to something?"

"Hard to say," his dad said. "She *was* very firm about the idea."

"Okay, stop," Jack said. "You're not the worst parents in the world. It was a good try. And . . . I appreciate the thought you put into it." At least that part was true.

"Jack's right," his mom said. "There's bound to be worse parents. It's a big world out there. It's nearly impossible to be the worst at anything."

"Excellent way to look at it," his dad said. "I'll venture we can only go up from here. With determination, we can crawl our way up to the middle of the pack."

• • •

The streets of downtown Nairobi teemed with *matatus*—minibuses covered in graffiti-style artwork and advertisements. On the sidewalks, men and women in suits swerved around each other. Hawkers peddled cigarettes and gum. A man with sharp shins sat cross-legged next to a wooden box overflowing with dried herbs. Young boys in faded T-shirts chased after tourists, tugging on sleeves and asking for shillings. Roasting meat and husks of corn smoked atop charcoal grills.

The taxi pulled in front of a three-story cement building.

"The Baobab Inn," the driver said.

"You actually made reservations this time," Jack said. "That's really an improvement. Good job, Mom and Dad."

His mom dug around her purse and muttered, "We were bound to forget something."

"So, you didn't make reservations?" Jack said.

"Baby steps, Son," his dad said.

The taxi driver muttered, "*Wazungu.*"

• • •

After a long conversation with the hotel manager, during which Jack's parents denied being the same Berensons who had left Mr. and Mrs. Grady to fend off the baboons of Lake Nakuru, they took two rooms with a connecting door. Jack ordered room service while his parents went out to rent a car.

A man named Samuel brought Jack a cheeseburger and a frosty Coke in a green glass bottle.

Samuel set the tray down, and Jack said, "Sir, have you been to the Rift Valley?"

"Yes, of course," Samuel said. "Many times."

"Is it hard to find?"

Samuel smiled and handed Jack the receipt to sign. "The Rift Valley would be hard to miss."

Jack signed his name and handed it back.

Samuel took the receipt, and his smile disappeared. "Berenson?" he said. He pocketed the receipt and stared at Jack. "Are you here to lead a safari?"

"Us?" Jack said. "No, we're not doing any safaris."

"That is good," Samuel said. "Nobody in the Rift Valley would be happy to see *those* Berensons."

Jack gulped.

"Our safari trade has just recovered from *those* Berensons. We can only hope the Gradys have recovered as well."

"They sound awful," Jack mumbled.

• • •

Jack's parents returned late in the afternoon.

"Great news, Jack," his mom said, "We rented a Jeep. Your dad and I went wild, planning. You would have been impressed."

"Just so," his dad said. "Right down to kicking the tires. I even kicked the spare tire. It was a regular military operation. The fellow at the rental company was gobsmacked."

Jack's mom saluted his dad. "A victorious campaign, General Berenson." She turned to Jack. "I told the clerk that while he might not see this keen eye for detail every day, we are the Berensons. We don't muck about."

"Did you get a spare gas can?" Jack asked.

"Jack, really. As if we would forget that after what happened on the island. Of course we got one," his mom said.

"Did you fill it up with gas?" Jack asked.

His mom snorted. "The idea that we would . . . to just have an empty container in the car . . . too ridiculous . . . " She glanced at Jack's dad. "Richard, you said you needed to step out?"

"Did I? Yes! Yes, I certainly did. I'll meet you at the restaurant as soon as I—"

"Get gas," Jack said, folding his arms.

"Get the petrol," his dad muttered.

• • •

Jack and his mom crossed Kimathi Street, dodging *matatus* blaring loud music. Dusk had settled over the city. The sweet scent of wood smoke hung in the air. Jack remembered it from the Caribbean—mosquito coils beginning to smolder.

The restaurant was named the Thorn Tree Café, which Jack thought was very sensible since there was a giant tree growing in the middle of it. People had posted notes around the trunk about safari trips for sale, shared rooms on the island of Lamu, trips to Uganda to see mountain gorillas, and backpackers wanting to find someone they had once traveled with but had lost track of somehow. A number of people looked for a girl named Davita, who appeared to be popular and elusive at the same time. A "Gary" had left three notes asking if she wanted to go to Lake Turkana.

"Isn't it brilliant, Jack?" his mom said. "Just imagine, a thorn tree has stood in that spot for at least a century. Ernest Hemingway himself was here."

Jack would never understand backpackers. Or Ernest Hemingway. Why did they traipse all over the planet when they could pick one safe, clean location and stay there? It was madness.

Jack's dad threw himself into a chair. "Every last-minute detail has been accounted for."

"Like the gas?" Jack said.

"Exactly," his dad said.

"Let's have a toast," Jack's mom said, holding up her Tusker beer. "Rift Valley, the Berensons are heading your way. Here's to having a wonderful adventure."

Jack raised his iced tea. "A wonderful, *safe* adventure."

"Safe as a Boy Scout," his mom said.

"Safe as milk," his dad said.

"Safety doesn't happen by accident," his mom said.

"Better safe than sorry," his dad said.

"Okay," Jack said, "it's great that you memorized some safety quotes. But it's more important to practice safety, not just talk about it. Did you write a safety measures checklist for us to follow?"

Jack's dad grabbed a menu and stared at it. His mom said, "That's on our list of lists we need to make. Only I can't find that list. But we did write up an equipment checklist. So that's something."

"That's definitely a step in the right direction," Jack said. "I'll write the safety checklist, but sooner or later you'll have to learn how to write one on your own."

CHAPTER 4

In which history repeats itself in new and exciting ways

The Berensons packed the Jeep at dawn. Soft pink light seeped into the avenues and alleys of the city. Security guards stood grimly outside darkened shops while stray dogs stretched out on the sidewalks.

As the Jeep wound through the quiet streets, Jack pulled out the safety checklist he had worked on the night before. "Are you ready?" he asked.

"We're all ears, Son. Fire away," his dad said.

"Okay. One: no fast driving. Dad, I mean you especially. Two: watch out for dangerous animals. Three: check the gas gauge every hour, and don't let it get under a half tank. Four: use SPF 55 sunscreen and reapply often. Five: try not to make anybody mad. It's best if you just don't talk to anybody or only say '*Asante sana.*' That's Swahili for 'thanks a lot.' Six: follow the map carefully. Seven: don't accidentally leave anybody at a rest stop. We don't want a repeat of the Grady incident."

Jack's mom raised her travel mug of tea over her head. "Got it, Jack."

"Dad?" Jack asked.

"Inspiring checklist," his dad said. "Heaps to remember, as usual."

"That's why I wrote it all down. You can read it as many times as you want," Jack said. "And remember that we have to follow the family decision-making rules too."

The Jeep sped by small farmsteads, their neatly tended sections forming a green and brown patchwork across the landscape. They turned west onto a road bordered by tall trees.

Jack bounced around in the backseat. "Not so fast, Dad," he said. "We don't want to get into an accident. Remember item one on the checklist."

"No worries, Son. Look around: who would we hit?"

"You never know," Jack said. "Remember when you almost hit that deer in Pennsylvania? A zebra might gallop right in front of us."

"I can see why you're going to Harvard someday, Son," his dad said. "About the last thing I was worried about was hitting a zebra."

Jack's mom had a map stretched across her lap and was tracing a route with her finger. "Richard, if we follow this road for about ninety-five kilometers, we'll hit a market town. We can top off the petrol and then head south."

"Got it," his dad said.

Jack really hoped they had some idea of where they were going. "Where's that book about Kenya you bought at the airport?" he asked.

"In the brown leather bag right next to you, Jack. How's that for organization?"

Jack was a little surprised. "Nicely done, Mom."

Jack pulled the book out and went to the index to find the valley where Meticiki lived. As he read about it, his intestines began tying themselves into knots.

"Hey," Jack cried, "do you have any idea how big this Rift Valley is? You can see it from space!"

"No worries, luv," his mom said. "We're not going to roam around the Rift Valley without a plan. We're not idiots. We know exactly where Meticiki lives. He's near the Mara."

• • •

The Jeep rolled into a bustling town, driving through streets filled with passersby and swerving bicycles. Jack had rested his elbow along the Jeep window but pulled it back in after getting clipped by a *matatu*.

The Jeep dodged a stray dog and swerved around a corner. "There's the market," his mom said.

Jack's dad pulled the Jeep into the dusty parking lot, squeezing in between a bus and a beat-up Toyota. They jumped out of the Jeep and weaved around crowds of people, following

narrow passageways through the market. Jack thought the crowded stalls were a stroke of genius. It was like having a hundred restaurants all in the same place. He and his parents ate spicy beef samosas, corn on the cob, and fried chicken. They bought a heaping plate of *nyama choma*, which, Jack discovered way too late, was goat meat.

Finally, they bought a cut-up pineapple, hopped in the Jeep, and filled the tank with gas. Jack's stomach stuck out like he had just finished Thanksgiving dinner. As the miles passed, the sun beat down on his head, and his eyelids grew heavy.

• • •

Jack woke to vast grasslands. Flat-topped trees that looked as if they had been replanted upside down covered the landscape. His mom stood on her seat, holding on to the top of the windshield and shading her eyes.

"Hello, sleepyhead," she said to Jack. She pointed to a dirt track on the left side of the road. "There's the turn, Richard."

"Hold on, Jack," his dad said. "It's about to get bumpy."

• • •

"Well," Jack's mom said as they bounced over the potholed track, "this is a rough road. Good thing we rented a Jeep and not a compact!"

"Who are they?" Jack asked, pointing at a line of men, dressed in red cloth robes, jogging along the path toward the Jeep.

"Ah," his mom said. "They're Maasai. You can tell by the *shukas* they're wearing."

His dad pulled the Jeep to the side of the path as the men approached. "*Jambo bwana hakuna matata asante sana*," he called.

The men stopped in front of the Jeep and stared. Jack did not think they looked very impressed with his dad's Swahili.

One of them said, "Are you lost?"

"Not a bit," his mom said. "We're the Berensons. We're never lost."

The group of men whispered to each other. "Berenson? No! It cannot be."

"We're just on our way to find our old friend

Meticiki," Jack's dad said.

"Do you know him?" his mom asked.

The youngest man opened his mouth to speak, but one of the older men laid his hand on the boy's shoulder and said, "Meticiki has not been seen. Anywhere. By anyone. For many months."

Another one said, "That is correct. He has moved. Very far from here."

"Yes," a third man said. "Meticiki has gone to Tanzania."

"Now that can't be right," Jack's dad said. "The last thing our pal would do was move without sending us his new address."

"Richard," his mom said, "they're probably thinking of some other Meticiki."

"Bound to be it."

One of the older men said, "You should not go this way. It is dangerous. There is a bull in *musth* to the south."

Jack flipped to the guidebook's glossary and looked up *musth*: "a periodic condition resulting in highly aggressive behavior, thought to be caused by hormonal fluctuations."

"We should do what they say," Jack said.

"You should turn back," the eldest of the Maasai said with a shrug. Then they jogged away down the track.

"They're a funny bunch," his dad said.

• • •

The Berensons drove along the dirt track, past three giraffes nibbling on the high branches of a tree.

"Look, Jack," his mom said, "they're eating acacia. That's what we'll use for the *enkang*. Giraffes don't mind the thorns, but lions do."

"Hold on, everybody," Jack's dad shouted. "Detour ahead!"

Jack just had time to grip the armrest before his dad swerved off onto the grassland. A massive bull stood in the middle of the track, staring at the Jeep. They veered around the animal, bouncing over the rough ground. Jack's dad waved at the bull and said, "Hi there, big fella."

The animal lowered its head and pointed its horns at the Jeep.

"Dad," Jack said, "that could be the bull in musth the Maasai warned us about. Don't make him mad."

"Nonsense," his dad said, driving the Jeep past the animal and swerving back on the track. "Your mom and I have been to Pamplona, remember? We ran the bulls, once upon a time."

His mom parted her hair, revealing a jagged scar. "Only sixteen stitches."

"That is an organized festival with ambulances and policemen," Jack said. "This is the wilderness, full of wild animals. It's not the same."

As they left the bull behind, fat drops of rain began to splash on Jack's head. "Hey," he said, "let's pull over and put the top up."

"Jeeps don't have tops, luv," his mom said.

"Yes, they do."

"Oh." Jack's mom twisted in her seat and said, "Then what I meant was, *this* Jeep doesn't have a top. Was that on the checklist?"

"No," Jack muttered.

Jack stuffed the guidebook in his pack. The track had turned to slick, brown mud, and the

Jeep splashed in and out of potholes. Its back end fishtailed as Jack's dad gunned the engine.

Jack's dad pressed harder on the gas. The wheels spun and dug deeper into the mud. It sounded like they were going a hundred miles an hour, except the vehicle was stationary.

"I don't suppose we have a roadside assistance plan," Jack said.

"No worries, Jack," his dad said, "your mom and I have been stuck in the mud before. And this time, we've got no corrupt policemen to bribe and no irate Hungarian townspeople to fend off. We'll have this sorted in a jiff."

Jack scanned the horizon. There were no other vehicles moving across the savannah, just a herd of grazing gazelle. They had left the bull far behind, and it had moved off the track to graze.

The gazelle picked their heads up, then bolted in unison, racing across the plain.

"Did you see that?" Jack asked.

"Magnificent," his mom said.

"Not magnificent!" Jack cried. "They are running! What are they running from?"

"Us, no doubt," his mom said.

There was a predator nearby, Jack thought. Probably a lion. Probably an army of lions.

He had watched enough Animal Planet to be acquainted with Mother Nature's ruthless personality. Mother Nature did not care if you were a person and had a whole life to live. She was all about survival of the strongest. Jack looked down at his arms. He was still what people called wiry.

"We should get away from . . . whatever those gazelle want to get away from," Jack said. He pointed to a stout tree nearby. "Look, right over there. We could climb that tree, hang around until the rain stops, and then push the car out of the mud."

"No need for that, Jack," his mom said. "Look." She pulled out three mini-umbrellas and handed one to him. "Thinking ahead again. The moment I noticed the Jeep didn't have a top, I thought, 'Hold on a minute, Claire. That's a minor detail. Exactly the kind of thing Jack gets so wound up about. So what would Jack do?' And here we are with umbrellas."

"That's great, Mom."

Jack's mom fist-bumped his dad.

"But getting wet is the least of our problems," Jack said. "We're surrounded by wild animals. If you find yourself in the jaws of a lion, it won't help you to have an umbrella."

"I'll tell you what, Son. Since you're determined to be in a tree, go ahead up and scout the horizon," his dad said. "See if you can spot the perfect location for our camp. Something with a view."

Something with a view? There was nothing *but* view.

Jack grabbed his pack and jogged over to the tree. He wished his parents had decided to follow him, but he had no intention of getting mauled by a lion because of their bad choices.

Behind him, his dad said, "Claire, our son becomes more boylike by the day. He insists on climbing the nearest tree, like any other rough-and-tumble scamp."

Jack paused and peered up into the tree. Its lower branches were thick and bare, but the higher branches were thinner and covered with leaves and thorns. An acacia tree. Jack hoped he wouldn't have to deal with any marauding giraffes while he was scouting the horizon.

His fingers grazed the bottom of the lowest branch. He jumped and tried to get ahold of it, but he missed and fell down.

"Have another go, Son. You're more athletic than you look," his dad called from the Jeep.

Jack scrambled to his feet and looked around. A log lay near the base of the tree. He rolled it under the branch, then stood on it. He grabbed the branch, wrapped his legs around it, and pulled himself up.

"Good show!" his mom called.

Jack waved to her and climbed higher. The gazelle stood still, ears pricked.

Rain continued to pour on the plains. The savannah stretched out in most directions as far as Jack could see, dotted with trees and brush. A low, rocky ridge stood to the east.

Jack could not imagine building a vacation camp in the middle of this wilderness. Where would they get groceries? What about the cow they were supposed to need? What if this Meticiki person didn't want to help them? And what if his parents didn't build the *enkang* the right way and a lion got in?

Hold on. Maybe that was too dramatic. After all, what had really happened? The car was stuck in the mud. Not exactly a life-threatening emergency. It was the kind of thing that could happen anywhere.

Jack took in a long, deep breath. Now that his heart had stopped pounding, he could even see the humor in the situation. Jack could imagine telling Diana the story. "Can you believe it? There we were, stuck in the middle of the savannah, and my parents just sat in the Jeep with umbrellas." Jack smiled as he imagined her laughing.

A movement across the eastern ridge caught his eye. Three large spotted cats stood on the rocks, each looking a different direction.

"Mom, Dad! Look on the ridge! Leopards! Three of them!"

His parents jumped up on their seats. "Ah! Those are cheetahs, Son," his dad said.

"Whatever!" Jack cried.

"How wonderful," his mom called. She

pulled out a pair of binoculars from the glove compartment.

A pounding sound filled the air. Jack bent down and peeked through the acacia branches.

The bull they had swerved around was thundering down the track toward the Jeep.

"Dad! Mom! Watch out!"

"Don't be silly, Jack," his mom said. "They're only cheetahs."

"It's that bull!" he yelled.

Jack's parents whipped their heads around.

The bull slammed into the truck, then skidded to a halt, watching the vehicle skate across the muddy track. Jack's dad clutched the roll bar. His mom grabbed at the top of the windshield while the binoculars spun out of her free hand. The mini-umbrellas sailed off in different directions.

The Jeep careened off the path and onto the grass, slowing to a stop. Jack's dad jumped down into his seat and threw the truck in gear.

The Jeep lurched forward, Jack's dad steering it toward Jack's acacia tree. The bull lowered its head.

"Jump in, Son," Jack's dad shouted, swerving underneath the lower branches.

"What?" Jack cried.

The Jeep made a wide U-turn.

"We're coming back around," his mom called.

The bull charged forward and galloped after the Jeep. Jack's dad hit the mud at full speed, fishtailed, and then bounced onto the grassland.

The Jeep barreled toward the tree. "Jump!" his mom yelled.

"I can't," Jack said.

The bull clipped the back bumper. The bumper rose in the air, bags and boxes spilling out onto the ground. The Jeep righted itself, facing away from the tree, and sped onto the open grassland.

Jack's mom stood on the seat, hanging on to the roll bar. "No worries, Jack," she shouted. "We'll be back to collect you directly!"

"Directly!" his dad shouted.

The Jeep zigged and zagged across the savannah, the bull galloping after it, until it began to look like a Matchbox car. It rounded a stand of trees and vanished over the horizon.

Jack watched his parents disappear. He wondered if, in all of their travels, his mom and dad had been cursed by a crazed witch doctor somewhere. Maybe they were walking around with dozens of curses on them. For all he knew, Mrs. Grady had made Berenson voodoo dolls and was sticking pins into them at that very moment. There had to be some logical explanation for why things always went so wrong.

Had Jack made sure there was plenty of gas in the Jeep? Yes. Had he imagined the Jeep would be speeding across the savannah with a bull chasing it? No. As his dad liked to say, live and learn.

Jack assumed his parents would eventually lose the beast. As soon as that happened, they would start rescue operations. But if the last time Jack got stranded was anything to go by, he'd be lucky if he didn't miss college because he was still sitting in a tree in Africa.

Jack crouched on the lowest branch and looked toward the ridge. The cheetahs were gone. They had probably called a meeting about how to sneak up on him. In a few moments, the rain let up and steam began to rise from the ground. Jack opened his pack. Maybe he had something he could use as a weapon. Next time he was in a car with his parents, he would bring a rifle. And maybe some hand grenades. He had:

- the travel guide
- his water bottle
- a small brown bottle with a picture of a dead bear on it (he had not packed that)
- a slim paperback titled *Seventh Grade in an Hour* (Jack had not packed that either, and he had a sinking feeling that was what his mom had meant by coming home "ahead of his schoolmates")
- a blank notebook with a pen (once again, had not packed that)
- and Mack the stuffed monkey.

Jack pulled the monkey out of the pack. "I could have told you gnoming was a bad idea."

Where were his phone and T-shirts and

insect repellent? And what happened to the SPF 55 sunscreen he bought?

Then it dawned on him. He had left his parents in charge of the equipment list. And they had reorganized the bags.

"Why?" he cried.

In which Jack's lifelong dream of having a tree house finally comes true

A crumpled piece of paper lay at the bottom of Jack's pack. He smoothed it out against a tree branch. The note had lines in both of his parents' handwriting, as if they had taken turns, and it was covered with scribbles and cross-outs and more scribbles. His mom had printed *EQUIPMENT CHECKLIST* across the top. Most of the page was illegible. What Jack could make out read:

> *Bear repellent—sprinkle on bear's face. Then run. (Do NOT forget Jack!)*

Notebook and pen—document rise of Berenson camping empire.
Seventh Grade in an Hour—J can speed-read and finish in a half hour.
Chips Ahoy—Sneak into house. (Avoid lecture from J about empty calories)

Jack supposed he should just be grateful that no actual bears resided in Kenya. And that his parents had reminded themselves not to leave him behind if they were suddenly attacked by one.

Jack's hand shook as he put the list back in his pack. He willed himself to relax. It was important not to overthink the situation. Jack knew that when he overthought a problem, he never imagined all the amazing miracles that could occur, only the unlucky chain of events that might eventually lead to death. Right then, he just had to do what needed to be done and hope he wouldn't be lost in the Rift Valley for very long.

After checking in every direction to be sure the cheetahs weren't creeping around, Jack climbed down from the tree. Considering what he had found in his own pack, he was almost afraid to examine the bags and boxes that had flown out of the Jeep.

The rain-soaked cardboard of the first box fell apart in his hands. Bright blue packages of Chips Ahoy! cookies plunked to the ground. Empty calories, located.

The second box had a variety of items, including an automatic barbecue lighter, a book called *An Idiot's Guide to Building Mud Huts*, six rolls of duct tape to hold the hut together, the walkie-talkies, a flashlight, and a pink dog leash with the word *Princess* spelled out in fake diamonds. Unless his parents had planned on adopting a Kenyan poodle, Jack had to assume that was for the cow.

Scattered on the grass, Jack found a fold-up tent stuffed into a nylon bag, the binoculars, two of the umbrellas, two rolled-up sleeping bags, a wooden crate of oranges, and a jerry can of water. Also nearby: a jar of Maxwell House instant coffee, a rain-soaked box of Earl Grey tea, and a gallon-sized ziplock bag of sugar. It looked as though his parents had planned for a lot of coffee breaks and teatimes.

The last box was white plastic with a snap lid. Its bold, red lettering read, *Property of The Mara Car Rental Company.* The box contained a screwdriver, pliers, a pair of work gloves, and a bag of rubber tire patches.

Jack ran his fingers over the flattened grass where the tires had run over the savannah. With the few hours of daylight he had left, he could gather supplies in his pack and go after the Jeep. But what if he ran into the bull and ended up gored to death?

Or what if it got dark and there was no tree to climb up? He'd be standing alone on the plains, able to see nothing but the glowing eyes of predators as they circled around him. The bloodthirsty animals would think, *Are you kidding me? He's just standing there?* Vultures would pick his bones clean by daybreak.

Maybe that was too dramatic. Jack examined the facts. He was alone, stranded somewhere in the Rift Valley in Kenya. His parents were last seen speeding across the plains ahead of an enraged bull; current whereabouts unknown. Three cheetahs were slinking around in the bush. To fend them off, Jack had . . . bear repellent.

No, he was not being too dramatic.

It would be safer to stay where he was. A search party might be setting out at that very moment. They would backtrack along the tire marks, and there he'd be, waving from the acacia tree. Or the Maasai warriors they had met might come jogging over the ridge.

Somebody would come along.

Jack dragged the crate of oranges under the lowest branch to stand on as a step stool. The dog leash had a loop on one end and a clip on the other. He threw the clip end over the low branch, threaded the clip through the loop, and pulled on it until the leash closed tight against the branch. Now that the leash was secured to the branch, he could use it to haul up supplies.

Jack forced open the leash's clip and attached it to the handle of the toolbox. He pulled himself up on the branch and then pulled the leash, with the toolbox attached, toward himself. After unclipping the toolbox, he dragged it to a higher branch.

For the next hour, Jack climbed up and down, clipping on a supply and pulling it up into the tree. He loaded his backpack with the smaller items. The jerry can was too heavy, so he rolled it under the shade of the tree. That just left the crate of oranges.

Sweat poured down Jack's cheeks as he lifted the crate, inch by inch. His arms ached. Finally, he grabbed the top and dragged it up. He propped the crate between the tree trunk and a limb growing up at a steep angle.

He surveyed his surroundings. It looked like a shipwreck in a tree.

Jack rearranged the dog leash so the loop handle hung a few feet off the ground. He would have to go down to the ground to fill his water bottle from the jerry can; the loop would give him a head start if he saw cheetahs running toward him.

Seated on the tree's lowest limb, Jack picked up the binoculars. Two tiny, deerlike creatures nibbled on the grass. A herd of zebra walked sedately across the savannah. The cheetahs had not returned to the ridge, but vultures circled over the rocky outcrop.

Jack put the binoculars down on the limb and craned his neck back, peering deep into the acacia branches. Thick and sturdy, they pointed in all directions. He would have to figure out a way to sleep in it without plummeting to the ground in the middle of the night. He could just imagine waking up in mid-flight and landing in the waiting jaws of a lion.

None of the branches were wide enough to sleep on. But he did have six rolls of duct tape. Jack supposed he could always duct tape himself to a limb for the night. Duct tape could hold fifty or sixty pounds. He had watched an experiment on TV that proved it. Jack was heavier than that, but he could always wrap it around twice.

A potential problem occurred to him. What if he got himself all taped up, then he couldn't get out quickly in an emergency? He didn't want to wake staring into the face of some predator.

Jack explored the acacia, examining the bigger branches and trying to think of another idea. He scrambled over to two branches on the right side of the tree. He jumped up and down on them. The limbs felt sturdy. And they ran almost straight beside each other. Maybe he could duct tape them together and put one of the sleeping bags on top.

Jack did the math. He had six hundred feet of tape. The tree limbs were about three feet apart. That meant he'd need at least six feet to go all the way around the two limbs one time. And for head-to-toe coverage, he'd have to go around, what, thirty times? Thirty multiplied by six was one hundred and eighty. Jack would have to go over it twice to be sure it would hold his weight. So that was three hundred and sixty feet. He had more than enough tape.

Jack slipped rolls of duct tape on his wrists like bracelets and began wrapping the tape around the first branch—three times, to serve as an anchor. Then he wound the tape around and around both branches. Jack worked his way through two rolls of tape, then worked his way back over the bed to reinforce the whole thing.

Once Jack had taped over everything twice, he laid one of the sleeping bags on top. He wound another roll of tape around the limbs, securing the bag in place.

Jack retrieved his backpack and carried it up to the duct tape bed. As long as he didn't jump up and down on it, which he had no plans of doing, he was confident the bed would hold.

The sun hung low in the western sky. There would only be another hour or so of daylight, Jack thought. He was near the equator, just as he had been while lost in the Caribbean. The sun didn't set at those latitudes; it fell down like a meteor.

Jack pulled the guidebook from his pack and lay on his bed. He flipped to a section titled "The Savannah."

The plains are the site of a great migration. Millions of wildebeest, zebra, and gazelle push forward on a never-ending quest for food and water. Predators trot close behind them, on a never-ending quest to kill the wildebeest, zebra and gazelle.

Africa's 'Big Five' are the elephant, the buffalo,

the rhinoceros, the lion, and the leopard. The fortunate traveler on safari may spot all of the 'Big Five' in one day.

"See them all in one day?" Jack whispered. "What kind of madman would want to see them all in one day?" Jack had forgotten rhinoceros even existed. They were like dinosaurs—the kind of creature a person might see in a museum, not running past the person in the wilderness. His hands shook as he thumbed through the book.

A half hour later, Jack discovered that a bull in musth was not the kind of bull he had been thinking of. It was a male elephant. Musth could be identified by black stuff running down either side of the animal's head.

The guidebook had other valuable takeaways. The bull that had chased the Jeep was actually a Cape buffalo, the most dangerous vegetarian on the planet. Lions worked in groups called prides and mainly hunted at night. Hyenas used their powerful jaws to take down prey and communicated through a series of distinctive calls. The honey badger might be small, but it was aggressive, fearless, and relentless. To escape from a charging rhinoceros, a person could jump into a body of water. But dangerous hippos might be in the water, so the person could also climb the nearest tree—and hope a leopard wasn't sitting in it. Cheetahs took down their prey at seventy miles per hour.

Jack fanned himself with the pages. He thought "the Big Five" didn't really tell the whole story. "The Big How Is Anybody Still Alive?" was more like it.

Jack slammed the book shut and stuffed it in his pack. The sun dropped below the horizon, and an eerie twilight settled over the plains.

In which Jack meets a few of the neighbors

The night rolled in like a black mist. Jack grabbed the binoculars and peered in every direction, hoping to see lights somewhere. If not the headlights of a rescue convoy, then the twinkling lights of a town. Or a campfire. Or a match. Some spark of light where he could direct signals from his flashlight.

Jack peered into the darkness, wondering if any lions nearby might slink out of their lair. He grabbed the stuffed monkey and looped its Velcro paws around a tree limb above his bed. If some wild animal thought about climbing up, hopefully Mack would fool it into thinking the tree was already packed with territorial primates.

"When I get home," Jack said, "I'm going to sign up for survival school."

The monkey swayed in the breeze, its black eyes staring blankly in the twilight. Trees across the savannah turned into giant hands reaching up from the earth.

A chill settled in the air. Jack reached for the extra sleeping bag and draped it over himself. Lying on the suspended duct tape bed, stars winking through the acacia leaves, he felt like he was floating in space.

High-pitched laughter erupted below.

Jack threw off the sleeping bag. "Hello!" he shouted. "Hello! Where are you?"

The laughter stopped.

Jack turned on his flashlight and waved it around. "I'm over here! Up in the tree!"

Another shriek of laughter pierced the night. From one direction, then another.

Jack paused. The laughs didn't sound right. Not like happy laughing—more like crazy laughing. The kind of laughing that would be in a horror movie at the exact moment the honeymooning couple realized they shouldn't have rented a remote cabin with no phone service.

More laughter came from Jack's right. Closer this time. His heart knocked against his ribs.

Jack whipped his flashlight toward a shuffling noise. An animal emerged from a stand of brush. Its silhouette looked like a dog's, except its front legs were longer than its hind legs.

A hyena.

The animal jerked its head away from the light, showing off its short, rounded ears. It raised its head and sent bloodcurdling laughter into the night.

Distant hyenas answered the call. Jack couldn't see them, but their laughs traveled back and forth like echoes in a canyon.

The calls grew closer. The hyena under Jack's tree turned. A larger hyena and two others met it near the stand of brush. They sniffed each other.

The largest hyena edged toward the tree and nosed the ground around the trunk. Another hyena pawed at the shredded cardboard box. A third pulled at the leash dangling from the tree limb.

The largest hyena stood on its hind legs, stretching its front legs up the trunk.

Jack didn't have hyena repellent, but bear repellent might work just as well. He grabbed the container out of his pack, pulled the extra sleeping bag over his head, and clicked on his flashlight to read the directions.

Bear-Bag: The number-one-selling synthetic bear urine, guaranteed to mimic the smell of real bears. Apply small drops of Bear-Bag to foliage and bring in the bears! Whether you hunt with a rifle or crossbow, Bear-Bag will be a staple on any trip.

Bring *in* the bears? It was supposed to repel them! He clicked off the flashlight. Apparently his parents had not read the fine print.

Jack twisted the top off while the largest hyena pawed at the acacia trunk. He leaned over as far as he dared and tipped the bottle. Nothing came out. He tipped it further and shook the container. Liquid poured out of the bottle all at once. It sprayed the hyena's face.

The hyena shook itself, then mashed its nose into the earth. The others sniffed the air and slowly backed away.

The lead hyena growled and shook its head back and forth, as if it were trying to cast off the scent. It bolted into the darkness. The rest of the pack chased after it.

Jack crouched on the limb, listening. Each time he heard a branch snap or leaves rustle, he clicked on his flashlight.

After a few hours, Jack's eyes felt heavy. He caught himself almost tumbling out of the tree.

He unhooked the dog leash, secured it to a branch near his bed, and clipped it onto one of his khakis' belt loops. If the duct tape holding up the sleeping bag gave way, he'd wake up dangling from the leash instead of getting mauled on the ground. Jack curled up in a ball and prayed for daylight.

• • •

The air warmed Jack's skin before he saw the sun. He was still in the bed. The tape had stretched and sagged a little, but it had not given way. Jack unhooked himself from the dog leash and grabbed the binoculars. The cheetahs were back on the ridge, stretched out on the rocks this time. Two giraffes loped by. No sign of the hyenas. Also no sign of a rescue vehicle.

Jack gulped down half a bottle of water and pulled the guidebook from his pack. As he browsed the book, a picture of a white stone building by the sea caught his eye. Two people stood in front of it, wearing flowing white robes and peaceful expressions. The place was a resort called Namaste For Kids, designed for families seeking peace and enlightenment. It specialized in activities like pottery making and yoga.

That was the kind of place his parents should build. Not a camp surrounded by wild animals. Nobody ever got charged by a buffalo or surrounded by prowling hyenas while they were making clay pots or stretching on a mat.

Jack pulled the foldout map of Kenya from the back of the book. He located the market town where they had stopped for lunch and then traced his finger south.

The route ended abruptly at a wide, green expanse. "The Maasai Mara," he cried. "That's what they meant when they said Meticiki lived near the Mara? Are you kidding me?"

Jack had thought Mara was a town. No wonder he'd been surrounded by hyenas. He was in the middle of a safari park.

Jack seriously wondered what kind of conversations his parents had when he wasn't around. "Well, darling," his dad might say, "the kid wasn't devoured by sharks like we planned—so what now?"

"How about the Maasai Mara, luv?" his mom would reply. "He'll be dead in an hour."

Jack stared at the map. A few tiny houses dotted the Maasai Mara. Safari lodges, according to the key. Jack made a rough guess at where he was and then used his pinky finger to measure the distance to the nearest lodge. It was the Mara Splendor Lodge, about three miles southeast. Even if he was exactly right about where he was, there was no way he could walk that far without getting mauled, gored, or trampled.

Jack was stuck until somebody came for him.

He had to do something about his defenses.

In which Jack fortifies the castle

Jack's stomach growled, and his head felt woozy. He ate a handful of cookies and an orange and then eyed the instant coffee. Jack had been meaning to try it for a while. When Zack's sister Kara turned eighteen, she had started drinking nonfat grande lattes from Starbucks. Jack wasn't sure what a latte was, but the green-and-white cups made her look casually confident.

He poured coffee and a big helping of sugar into his water bottle and shook it.

Jack guzzled the coffee and felt more alert. Then really alert. Then like electricity ran through his veins. He didn't feel casually confident, but he could see why Kara was always laughing.

Jack raised his bottle to Mack the monkey. "Cheers," he said. "It's so true what they say: things *do* look better in the morning. Especially when you have coffee."

A flash of movement caught his eye. The cheetahs had leapt to their feet. They bounded over the ridge and disappeared. The thought of predators creeping up the tree came back to him. Jack had seen his neighbor's cat, a fat tabby named Winston Churchill, climb trees. But every time Winston Churchill reached a branch, he couldn't get back down. The last thing Jack needed was to be trapped in a tree with a wild, supersized Winston Churchill. There had to be a way to keep the animals out.

Then he remembered the *enkang* his parents had planned to build to protect the camp from lions. If it could protect a person in a house, there was no reason it couldn't protect a person in a tree. At least, Jack hoped there was no reason.

He put on the work gloves and grabbed the

pliers. Now that he was up close to the thorns, he could see why the Maasai built fences with them. They were like sewing needles, an inch long with a sharp point.

Jack leaned out near a thin branch, grasped it with the pliers and twisted. What he really needed were hedge clippers. He supposed the Mara Car Rental Company had not imagined that one of their customers would need to build an emergency *enkang* in the middle of a fun-filled safari.

The thorns pricked his arms. He wrenched the branch free, threw it to the ground, and kept going.

Jack worked through the morning, taking a coffee break between every couple of branches.

"Well," he said, holding out his arms to Mack, who was still hanging from the branch over his bed. "I look like I have the measles, but I think I have enough raw material for a fence. Once I have it built, I can relax and wait to be rescued. Again."

Jack paused. How could his parents have lost him twice?

Jack's mom and dad had tried to follow the family rules. They had planned to hire Meticiki as a technical consultant for the camp, which was definitely closer to Jack's careful style of thinking. But it hadn't worked. Nobody would call being stranded in the Maasai Mara a success.

"Never mind," Jack said. "That *enkang* won't build itself."

Jack dragged the larger branches to the base of the tree and leaned them around the trunk. He had thought he would have to duct tape the branches together, but when he laid one branch on top of another, they naturally grabbed at each other. They also grabbed at him, snatching at his pants and T-shirt. He had so many holes in his clothes he looked like he had been attacked by a paper shredder.

Jack built the fence as high as he could reach and then built it outward. He stood back. There was no way anything could get through it.

He swung himself up on the dog leash and then pulled the leash up. The tree was as safe as a castle with a moat.

Settling himself on his bed, an orange in one hand and a couple of cookies in the other, Jack watched the afternoon sun filter through the leaves of the tree.

He wondered how often Diana ever thought about him. She had to think about him sometimes. She had sent the monkey on the trip, so naturally, when she thought about the monkey, she would think about who had it.

Diana was probably checking her mailbox for those amusing postcards Jack was supposed to send. She would end up thinking he was having such a good time hanging out with Maasai warriors that he couldn't be bothered. Maybe she would get so mad she would start hanging out with Zack. Or even worse, Ken Castleberry—Mr. My-Rich-Parents-Are-Going-To-Buy-Me-A-Car-When-I'm-Sixteen.

Jack pulled out the notebook and pen.

Hi Z—

You were right, I'm lost again. Parents were last seen driving across the plains with a buffalo chasing them. I survived the night by using bear bait to drive off a pack of wild hyenas. (My Mom and Dad packed it. Don't ask.) Today, I built an enkang *around the tree—it is the Maasai tribe's version of a moat. At least I am safe from predators. Have you tried coffee? It makes my hands shake, but except for that I love it. (Ask Kara to buy you some.) If you don't hear from me for a long time, don't assume I'm dead and start hanging out with Diana. I could turn up at any time. If I AM dead, and you are hanging out with Diana, I will haunt you as a ghost. If you see Ken Castleberry lurking around and talking about the car he doesn't have, tell him I am in Japan training as a black belt and turning myself into a deadly weapon.*

J.

Then he got to the hard one.

Diana—

Gnoming update: Mack is in a tree in the Maasai Mara. (I am with him.) I don't know if you will ever get this letter, but I did say I would write. Anyway, if I live, I was wondering if you want to be my girlfriend. Or if you already are, then I am just confirming that. Or if you're not and don't want to be, please don't tell anyone I asked even if you hear that I am dead. Also, don't believe what Ken Castleberry says about getting a car.

P.S. The monkey is doing fine.

How to sign off? *Love?* No! Then he thought about *sincerely*, *fondly*, *regards*, *sayonara*, *ciao*, *arrivederci*, *bye-bye*, *warmly*, *XOXO*, *all best*, and *truly yours*. Nothing sounded exactly right.

Finally, he wrote:

Catch you later . . . hopefully. Jack Berenson

Jack didn't have his phone, so instead of taking a gnoming picture, he sketched the monkey swinging from the tree branch.

As Jack slipped the notebook back into his pack, he noticed the other book his mom had brought on the trip. He cracked open *Seventh Grade in an Hour* and read the introduction.

Welcome to a brand new approach to learning. Folks, the U.S.A. is currently ranked seventeenth in education. This eye-opening statistic led the Learn It Quick Institute to conclude that pressuring a child into overachieving is not only pointless, but also highly annoying to the child. (A child determined to overachieve should move to Finland [# 1] and stop bothering everybody else.) This book is designed to provide the bare minimum, allowing the child to spend more time on activities such as video games and texting while still maintaining a chance of future employability. The child will find that when taking any test in the seventh grade, he or she can simply apply the information available within these pages. Booklets are available for grades K through 12, making it possible to complete an entire education in six and one-half hours. Let the education revolution begin!

Jack flipped through the pages. The book seemed to be one long list of phrases and figures:

.50 = 50%

Mr. Smith will use 8.5 gallons of gasoline

cold-icy

cold-hot

Charles Dickens

The variable is temperature

Marie Curie

O_2

photosynthesis

the Navajo

No wonder the authors thought a whole grade could be done in an hour. It was a list of answers. They had sped up the whole thing by not bothering with the questions. Jack shut the book and pulled out his letter to Zack.

P.S. Here's how my homeschooling is going. My only textbook is called 7th grade in an hour. It's a list of answers. Mr. Smith will use 8.5 gallons of gasoline. Where is he going? I don't know. I'm guessing you're finding that out right now.

• • •

Late in the afternoon, the tree was still a mess. Jack climbed to the other side, unfurled the dome tent, and tied the guylines at the base of the tent to different branches. The tent material formed a big fabric basket. Jack filled it with the oranges, cookies, coffee, and the bag of sugar. He dragged the empty orange crate over to his bed and propped it on a nearby limb as a bookshelf.

A sturdy branch stretched out ten feet above Jack's bed. Jack climbed up with the tire patches, the lighter, and a walkie-talkie. If he heard a search plane, he'd light the tire patches to make a smoke signal and use the walkie-talkie to amplify his voice while he shouted *Mayday*.

As the sun set, Jack stretched out on his bed. His arms and legs felt like jelly. He fell asleep listening to the cicadas take over the night.

• • •

At sunrise, Jack rolled over and peered at the base of the tree. The *enkang* was exactly as he had left it.

He jumped up. First thing, coffee and cookies. Jack grabbed his empty water bottle and scrambled down the dog leash.

Jack carefully tipped the jerry can, letting the water dribble into his bottle. It was half full when the air was filled with an overpowering smell. Noxious fumes assaulted his nose until he felt he was choking.

CHAPTER 8

In which an unscheduled gnoming trip takes place

Jack dropped the jerry can and turned toward the smell.

A black, solidly built animal with a white stripe down its back stood five feet away, staring at him. It looked like a skunk on steroids. But Jack knew it wasn't a skunk. He'd seen a picture of it in the guidebook. This was a honey badger. Aggressive, fearless, and relentless.

It growled.

Jack inched away from the badger. As he stumbled backward toward the dog leash, he tripped over a clump of grass and landed on his back. He scrambled to his feet. The animal moved closer.

Jack grabbed the leash. The animal sank its teeth into his pant leg. Jack swung back and forth on the leash, waving his leg to shake the badger off. The fabric gave way, and the animal fell to the ground.

Jack pulled himself up on the lowest limb and peered down at the badger. A shred of khaki hung from its mouth.

That was too close. Jack would have to be more careful when he was on the ground.

The animal circled the tree.

"Hah," Jack said. "I bet you didn't expect to find an *enkang*, did you?"

The badger pulled at the thorny branches.

"What are you doing?" Jack cried. "Stop that!"

The animal attacked the *enkang* with murderous abandon. It yanked and snarled and pulled branches apart. The thorns did not seem to have any effect on the badger at all.

Jack climbed up to his bed and looked over the edge. The badger had clawed its way through the *enkang* to the base of the tree. It gripped the bark with its powerful claws and scrambled upward.

The creature was deranged.

Jack inched farther out on his sleeping bag.

The badger leapt onto the opposite end of the bed. A low, steady growl erupted from its throat. The animal bared its teeth, showing sturdy white fangs.

Anything Jack could possibly use as a weapon was on the other side of the tree. He could jump to the ground, but even if he didn't break one of his legs, the insane animal would just run down the tree and chase him across the savannah.

The badger was going to tear him to pieces.

It took a step forward.

Mack the monkey swung in the breeze, hanging from a branch in front of Jack.

Jack grabbed the stuffed monkey and held it in front of him as a shield.

The badger lunged and sank its teeth into the monkey's body, ripping it from Jack's hands. The animal turned and sprinted down the trunk with the monkey in its jaws.

Looking down, Jack watched the badger slip through the opening it had made through the *enkang*. It jumped into the grass and clawed and bit the stuffed animal. The badger shook the monkey in its jaws like a dog with a bone, the tall grass bending as the animal raced across the savannah. Then it disappeared, as if the animal had dived underground.

Jack wiped the cold sweat from his face. He had congratulated himself that nothing could get into the tree. He had thought he was safe from predators. But he had been wrong.

At least he was alive. But now Mack the monkey was gone. How would he explain that to Diana? Jack was supposed to bring home interesting pictures of it posing in Africa. Now, if he arrived home at all, what was he going to say? "Oh, yeah, about the monkey. He went gnoming with a honey badger. Sorry 'bout that."

After checking in every direction, Jack swung down to the ground to fix the hole in the *enkang*.

At the base of the tree, he righted the

overturned jerry can. The cap was gone, and the ground around the can was wet—half the water had spilled out.

Jack rolled a handful of grass into a tight ball and stuffed it into the top of the jerry can. He climbed back up to his bed and duct-taped one of the tent poles until it stood completely straight and then taped the screwdriver to the end of the pole. He'd use it as a sword if the badger came back.

He grabbed the notebook off the shelf and added to his letter to Zack.

Correction. The acacia thorn moat does not protect me from EVERY predator. A honey badger broke through the enkang *this morning. Do not be fooled by the name—they are crazed and dangerous killers. They are also thieves. Diana made me take that stuffed monkey with me. I'm supposed to take pictures of it. (If you tell anybody, I will tell the whole school about how you left an anonymous note in Linda Carmichael's mailbox. I will even tell them WHAT IT SAID.) The last time I saw the monkey, the badger had it by the neck and was running across the grass with it. I might have to tell Diana that a pride of lions stole it.*

• • •

Jack lay on his bed, sipping water from his dwindling supply. He had decided that coffee was out from now on. He would only drink water, and as little of it as possible. The jerry can was only a quarter full, and he had no idea how many days he would have to make it last.

He mulled over his chances of somehow getting the monkey back. The only logical way he could imagine getting it back depended on his parents following the family rules. If they had done what they were supposed to do, then they'd driven directly to a police station to report a missing person. Sooner or later the area would be swarmed by police with high-powered rifles. Jack could casually mention that some of his personal property was in the badger burrow. Would they mind getting it for him?

But had his parents followed the rules?

Probably not. If they had been following the rules, they wouldn't have a missing person to report. They wouldn't have lost him in the first place.

His parents really had not put enough effort into trying to think the way Jack did. Once in a while they would do something he would do, but they weren't consistent. They hadn't made it a lifestyle.

Of course, Jack admitted, he hadn't been a stickler for the rules either. Jack had mostly just pretended he was more open to taking chances. He'd been secretly convinced that all magical transformations should happen on his parents' side.

But if he *had* been thinking more like them and less like himself, he wouldn't have climbed the tree. He would have stayed in the Jeep, and at this moment, they would all probably be at some restaurant, eating cheeseburgers and laughing about the crazy buffalo that had chased them for miles.

Climbing the tree had seemed like the safest option at the time, but look where it had got him.

If his parents had been chased up a tree by

a honey badger and had a valuable item stolen from them, what would they have done about it? Probably tackle the badger to the ground and then notice that one of their arms was racing across the savannah in the jaws of a wild animal.

Then his one-armed mom or dad would say something like, "No worries. We'll just pop over to the badger's burrow and collect that monkey directly. Nothing easier."

Jack had no intention of just "popping" over to the burrow of a wild animal.

But if he actually got the monkey back, he'd never have to mention anything about it to Diana. All he had to do was figure out what his parents would do, then scale it back until he arrived at a plan that allowed him to keep both of his arms.

If he were really going after the monkey, he would have to carefully map out a strategy. *If* he were going.

Going after Mack felt like the wrong thing and the right thing at the same time. Wrong because it wasn't anything he would normally do. Right because he was following the family rules.

Jack thought that if Diana were there, she'd say, "I had to pop ten water balloons to win him. Go get that monkey *right now*."

So it was decided. He was going to get that monkey back from the badger. Jack leaned over a branch and threw up.

In which Jack launches Operation Stun and Run

Jack wiped his mouth. Deciding to get the monkey back was one thing. Figuring out how to do it was another. He had to flush the badger out of its burrow and then prevent it from removing one of his arms while he got the stuffed animal out.

It would have to be a precise operation. Military style. Unfortunately, Jack was short on military training.

Jack climbed from branch to branch, examining all his supplies. He spent the remainder of the day trying to assemble an arsenal of weapons. Through trial and error, he discovered that it was not possible to turn one of the tent poles into an acacia-thorn-shooting blowgun, and he'd actually inflicted damage on himself with his efforts to create a suit of armor out of thorns and tape.

For a while, in the early afternoon, he had thought he'd figured out a plan. He would send one of the walkie-talkies into the burrow, duct-taping it to a thin branch and lowering it in like a fishing pole. Then he could shout something frightening into the walkie-talkie like, "Run for your life, badger!" But when Jack played that plan out in his mind, it always ended with the badger noticing who was holding the fishing pole and chasing him back to the tree.

As Jack sat on his bed, examining the extra sleeping bag he had been using as a blanket, he wondered if he could melt the metal on the zipper. Maybe he could make bullets and shoot them out of one of the tent poles—a bullet-shooting blowgun. He lit the barbecue lighter and held it against the zipper pull. The metal began to warm on his fingers. Jack peered down to see if it was melting, and fire shot up into the air. The heat slammed into Jack's face. The end of the sleeping bag burst into flames. Jack dropped the lighter and picked up the other end. He thrashed the burning bag against tree branches until the flames died down. The bag hung limp from his hands, smoldering black smoke at the other end.

"That can't be safe," he whispered.

Jack examined the half-burned sleeping bag and noticed the label sticking out on the side. *L.L. Keen—Made in Chinamalaynesia.* That wasn't even a real country. Where did his parents go shopping?

Jack rubbed his eyes. The place where his eyebrows should have been felt smooth. They were gone.

His parents had bought sleeping bags that could go up in flames in a matter of seconds! It was so like them. It was so dangerous. It was so . . .

Jack paused. Dangerous. He had been trying to build dangerous weapons all day. Maybe what he'd been looking for was right in front of him.

Jack pulled hunks of stuffing from the bag. He rolled them into a tight ball, then tied the nylon shell from one of the umbrellas around it. It would be the smoke bomb of all smoke bombs.

Jack worked through the rest of the day until finally he had an arsenal that might work. Maybe.

The rescue operation would launch at dawn.

• • •

Jack lay awake for hours, reviewing the plan. A voice in his head interrupted him at each step. *Don't do it. Don't do it. Don't do it.* He reminded himself that it was the same voice that had told him to climb a tree. Where he had been living ever since. That voice in his head was exactly why he needed to follow the Berenson Family Decision-Making Rules.

As the sky turned pink, Jack downed some water and geared up.

Jack knew he couldn't count on being able to scare the badger away. As he had found out already, honey badgers didn't get scared away.

He had to trap the animal, at least long enough to get Mack the monkey back.

The honey badger trap he had made the day before was already on the ground. He had taken what was left of the nylon from the burned sleeping bag and tied off any holes the fire had made. The bag was zipped up on either side, with an opening at the end that was big enough for the badger to pass through. Jack had pried off the top slats of the orange crate, leaving an open square, like a picture frame. He had pulled the nylon around the wooden square, keeping the entrance wide open.

Just in case his trapping plan fell through and he found himself in combat, Jack had fashioned a slingshot out of a Y-shaped tree branch and an elastic band he had slid out of the stitching of his backpack. Now, he slipped it in his pocket, along with a handful of rocks.

Jack set the stuffed nylon smoke bomb on the ground and stuck the lighter in his pocket. His backpack was already filled with cookies and a couple of oranges.

He grabbed the last item in his arsenal: a tent

pole, for grabbing the monkey. Jack had broken off a metal spoke from the umbrella, used the pliers to fashion it into a hook, and secured it to the end of the pole. He was ready.

The voice in his head said, *No. No. No.*

"Don't even start," he said.

Jack jumped down to the ground. The burrow was about a hundred yards from the tree. At the halfway mark, he paused and spread cookies and oranges in the grass. If the badger chased after him, hopefully food would distract the animal.

Staying as quiet as possible, Jack stepped forward. There it was. A big hole in the ground. Once he started the operation, there was no going back.

Jack lit the smoke bomb and dropped it in front of the den. He dragged the orange crate's frame and the attached nylon bag behind it. Growling erupted from inside the burrow.

The badger scrambled out through the smoke and into Jack's propped-open sleeping bag. Jack stomped on the frame inside the bag, collapsing it, and kicked it out of the way. Hands shaking, he struggled with the zipper as his captive flailed at the bag's opposite end.

Jack reached behind him and whipped out the tent pole. He fished it in the hole. Nothing. He got a sinking feeling that the badger had eaten the stuffed animal. He twisted around and then shoved his arm forward until he felt the pole push against something—hopefully not another badger.

The thrashing animal would rip and claw its way free in minutes. Jack wiggled the pole until he had hooked whatever was still in the hole. A brown Velcro paw inched its way into daylight.

Stuffing the monkey into his pack, Jack scrambled to his feet and ran. Halfway to the tree, he whipped around, ready to fire from the slingshot if the badger were on his heels.

The animal was still in the bag, but one claw had already ripped through the nylon.

Jack bolted to the tree and skidded to a stop at the dog leash. He pulled himself up onto the lowest limb, heaving.

"Done," he said.

Jack crawled up to his bed and grabbed the binoculars. The badger had worked its way out of the trap. It flung the nylon bag around in the dirt. It paused and raised its nose to the air, then ran to the scattered cookies, then back to thrash the bag, then toward the food, pouncing on an orange.

Jack pulled the monkey out of his pack. Its body slumped against a branch. The animal's brown polyester fur was streaked with dirt, and its insides had lost half their stuffing.

"I'll have some explaining to do," Jack said. "I better try to fix you up."

Jack pushed the stuffing back into Mack and then added some more stuffing from his sleeping bag. The monkey looked a little better, but Jack would have to be careful that nobody lit a match anywhere near it, as the stuffed animal was now filled with highly flammable material. One eye hung on by a thread. Jack pushed it back in and slapped tape around it to hold it in place.

After hanging the monkey from a branch, Jack examined his handiwork. The monkey's body was lumpy and uneven. The silver duct tape made the stuffed animal look like some kind of primate astronaut. Jack wouldn't be able to show the monkey to Diana until after he had bought it a T-shirt. And a pair of large sunglasses. But he had got the monkey back.

The badger ran from place to place, checking the ground for the cookies and oranges Jack had left scattered. Finally, it stomped back to its burrow.

Jack watched the badger disappear into its hole. Following the family rules had actually worked. Jack had thought like his mom and dad, added some safety features, and come up with a successful plan.

Except, even though he'd gotten Mack back, the whole rescue felt not exactly right. Like maybe he shouldn't have done it.

"Whatever," he said to Mack. "That's just the voice in my head talking."

• • •

Jack sat on his bed, squinting into his binoculars. He figured he probably had another four days of water left if he was careful. Hopefully, somebody would come and get him before then. Another rainstorm would fill up the jerry can, but he couldn't count on that. Jack had noticed that Mother Nature hardly ever did anything for his convenience.

A lone elephant lumbered over the ridge, swinging its head from side to side as if it were trying to dislodge a bug from its ears. The animal paused in front of a spindly tree, lowered its head, and charged. The tree fell under the weight of the beast. The elephant circled back around and stomped on it.

What was the animal doing? Beating up a tree seemed pretty pointless. Unless . . .

Unless that was the elephant bull in musth the Maasai had warned about.

The elephant continued on its path, shaking its head. At least it had decided to go the other way. The last thing Jack needed was an elephant with a hormone problem thundering around the neighborhood. He focused the binoculars back to the ridge. Beyond the rise, a red-and-yellow-striped balloon sailed across the blue sky.

Jack sat up. People! People in a balloon!

"Hey!" he cried, leaping up. "I'm over here!"

Jack scrambled up to the signal post. He fumbled with the lighter until a flame sprang up. He held it to the tire patches. Black smoke billowed from the burning rubber in his hand. He held it over his head and crawled up as high as he dared. Waving the smoking patches, he yelled into the walkie-talkie. "Over here! Mayday, Mayday, Mayday! Jack Berenson calling a Mayday."

The flames burned through the patches, toward Jack's fingertips. He dropped them on a branch, and they smoldered out.

"Mayday," Jack shouted, grabbing the binoculars. The balloon was about a quarter mile northeast. It had drifted past his tree before he had even seen it. Now it continued on its course, farther and farther away. He had been sure black smoke and the walkie-talkie would attract attention. What would it take? A rocket launcher?

Sweat poured down Jack's forehead. His lungs burned from the acrid smoke. Coughing, he wiped his face with his T-shirt. Black smudges streaked across the shirt like tire marks on a road.

Jack supposed the balloon was full of tourists on safari. His guidebook said that people liked to float over the animals and then land and have a champagne breakfast.

He hoped they were enjoying their eggs.

• • •

The next morning, there was still no sign of rescue vehicles. Or the rain that would fill up the jerry can.

Jack took inventory. He had plenty of cookies. Seven oranges still lay at the bottom of the tent basket. He scrambled down to the jerry can. The ball of grass he had used as a top had fallen in. Clumps floated through the brownish water—there was maybe an eighth of the can left. Tiny droplets clung to the inside walls of the container.

Jack had thought he would have enough water for four days, but now, it looked like he'd lost half of his supply to the heat.

But what did it matter if Jack had enough

water for four days or two days? If his parents had launched a rescue effort, someone would have shown up already. Had his parents reported a missing person? Or had they flown back to Pennsylvania and hired a psychic to reveal his location? Either one was a possibility.

Jack scrambled up the tree and ripped off a square of duct tape to cover the top of the jerry can. What were his options? The water was contaminated, and it wasn't going to last very long. If nobody was coming for him, he would have to find a way out himself.

His best chance was flagging down another balloon. He'd seen one. Surely he'd see another. Jack grabbed the guidebook. An ad on the back promoted the Mara Splendor. That was the lodge on the map that Jack thought was the closest to where he was. The balloon he had seen had to be from there. The ad even showed one drifting across the sky. The lodge sent up a balloon every other day at dawn, so guests could experience the grandeur of the savannah from a bird's-eye view. That meant the next one could come as soon as the following morning.

The people in the first balloon hadn't heard Jack shouting from the tree, but what if he could get right under the balloon's path? He could slingshot one walkie-talkie up toward it and shout Mayday into the other one. They'd have to hear him. All he had to do was use the binoculars to spot the next balloon and then run like crazy until he was underneath it.

Jack looked up the Mara Splendor Lodge in the guidebook. He felt almost giddy reading about the place. Guests of the lodge enjoyed ultramodern accommodations, fine dining, and a sophisticated wine list. Fine dining would be a nice change from cookies.

• • •

That afternoon, Jack organized his pack. It couldn't be too heavy; he'd need to move quickly. Oranges, in case he didn't make it and ended up spending the night in another tree somewhere. The slingshot and walkie-talkies. Binoculars. His notebook. The monkey. He would fill his pockets with rocks for the slingshot in case a wild animal began to stalk him. Hopefully it wouldn't come to that.

Darkness settled on the savannah. The cheetahs had not returned to the ridge, and there was no sign of the badger. The air was still as the last light of the sun disappeared.

Jack settled onto his bed and whispered, "One more night to get through. Then I am on my way home."

That night was hotter than the previous ones had been. Sweat poured from Jack's forehead. His throat was scratchy and dry, but he was saving the last of the water for the morning, when he would need all his strength. When he got to the Mara Splendor Lodge, he would drag a chair into the shower, turn the cold water on, and sit there. He might even order from the wine list while he was sitting in the shower. Now that he was a coffee drinker, he should probably find out what else he had been missing.

Jack tossed and turned through the night. In the predawn light, he climbed down to the ground and finished the water from the jerry can. The liquid tasted like dirt, but it took away the dry feeling in his throat. Jack used an acacia thorn to pin a note to the base of the tree before he climbed back up.

If you are searching for Jack Berenson, IT'S ABOUT TIME! I have gone to flag down a balloon to take me to the Mara Splendor Lodge. I will be registered under the alias Jack Beren. (Due to the 'Grady incident,' I'm afraid to use my real name.)

Jack scrambled up to the signal post to watch for the balloon. The voice in his head said, *You want to run across the plains and then shoot a walkie-talkie into the air with a slingshot? Are you kidding me? That will never work.*

"Cut it out," he replied.

• • •

As gray dawn gave way to a pink, streaked sky, the red and yellow balloon appeared on the horizon.

"All I have to do," Jack said, climbing down, "is get around the honey badger's lair, not run into any hyenas, avoid the elephant that beats up trees—and every other member of the Big Five—and I'll be fine."

A blaring, flat, trumpeting sound broke the silence. “Roowwrrhh.”

A gray behemoth charged across the grassland, heading straight for the tree. It looked like an apartment building on four legs.

CHAPTER 10

In which Jack makes like a wildebeest and migrates

Jack swung himself back up into the tree and hugged the trunk, bracing himself.

The tree trembled with the impact, shaking Jack's teeth. The elephant stood at the base, its forelegs crunching the acacia branches. The elephant backed up. A branch from the *enkang* was stuck onto one of its legs, but it didn't seem to notice.

Jack scrambled higher. The animal lumbered around to the other side of the tree.

The elephant was nearly eight feet tall and twenty feet long. Long white tusks stretched out in front of its face. Its massive ears flapped back and forth like gray sails.

Dark streaks ran down both sides of its head.

The bull in musth.

The elephant lumbered underneath Jack's tent basket. It lifted its trunk, and boxes of cookies fell to the ground.

The balloon was approaching fast. If he wasn't running toward the ridge in the next few minutes, he'd never make it.

Jack climbed down to the lowest branch. If he were careful, he might be able to slip away unnoticed.

The elephant's head turned in Jack's direction.

Jack scrambled back up the tree, seizing one of the higher branches as the animal knocked itself against the trunk.

The elephant went back to the tent basket and tore at it until it was in shreds.

Jack's eyes stung. He couldn't fight off an elephant. It was one thing for life to throw a couple of surprises at a person, but the surprises should be spread around more equally. There

were probably people all over the world who hadn't had a surprise in weeks. Why didn't life go see *those* people?

Jack took a deep breath. What would his parents do? Probably jump on the elephant's back and try to ride it to the lodge. So that was out.

The elephant paused at the orange peels Jack had thrown to the ground. The beast picked up each peel and deposited them one by one in its giant mouth.

Jack pulled an orange from his pack and threw it in the opposite direction of the ridge. The elephant turned at the sound of the plop. It lumbered to the orange, picked it up, and ate it.

The balloon was moving fast. Jack had to go.

He put on his backpack and crept down to the lower branches. He stood on a branch, loaded the slingshot with an orange, and yelled, "Hey! Watch this!"

The orange sailed over the elephant's head and rolled into the brush. The animal wheeled around and tramped after it.

Jack jumped down from the tree and ran.

He flew by the burrow—no sign of the

badger. No cheetahs on the ridge either. Jack scrambled up the slope.

Herds spread across the valley below. Everywhere Jack stared, bearded wildebeest grazed, looking like a thousand grandfathers. Gazelle stood in groups while their babies hopped and chased each other. Two zebra stood still, each resting its head on the other animal's back. Thousands of animals stood right in the balloon's path.

The balloon began to sail over the wildlife. Jack couldn't turn back. The only thing waiting for him at the acacia tree was a killer elephant. Yes, there were a lot of animals below. But they were herd animals. No wildebeest or a zebra was out there thinking, *If I could only find Jack Berenson, I would kill him.*

Jack raced down the slope. If he could just casually run past the animals, acting like nothing unusual was happening . . .

The breeze blew toward Jack, and the musky smell of animals assaulted his nose. One by one, the wildebeests picked up their heads and looked in his direction.

The balloon floated farther north.

"Excuse me," Jack said, winding around a pair of wildebeests. "I'm in a hurry."

At the sound of Jack's voice, the wildebeests panicked. Some bolted away. Some bolted toward him. Arms pumping, Jack dodged three antelope.

As one group of animals saw another group running, it sprinted off, which caused the next group to bolt. The plains swirled with wild eyes, pounding hooves, and clouds of dust. A wildebeest crashed into Jack and sent him flying through the air. He landed with a thud on the grass. By the time he could stand again, most of the animals on the plains had slowed to a walk; some had even gone back to grazing.

The balloon sailed ahead of Jack, racing with the wind.

Running after it, Jack ripped the walkie-talkies out of his pack. He pinched one walkie-talkie in his armpit and fired the other one toward the sky with his slingshot.

With the walkie-talkie he'd held onto, Jack shouted, "Mayday!"

The second walkie-talkie had risen twenty feet in the air. It landed with a thud at his feet.

The voice in his head had been right. There was no way that plan could ever have worked.

The balloon continued its course, getting farther away by the second. Jack grabbed a rock from his pocket and took off after it. As he closed the distance, Jack recognized his dad's thick, black head of hair.

Jack aimed and fired.

His dad disappeared into the basket.

"Got you," Jack whispered.

Jack's mom bent down and reappeared holding Jack's dad upright. She looked down and pointed at Jack.

His dad rubbed the back of his head and yelled something Jack couldn't hear.

"Hurry up!" Jack cried.

The balloon blew ahead and then slowly lost altitude until it landed in a series of thumps.

Jack's parents jumped out and ran to him. His mom clutched him; his dad slapped him on the back. His dad said, "Clever thinking, knocking old dad off his feet like that."

"Jack," his mom said. "Here you are, you rascal." She stared into Jack's face. "Luv, what have you done with your eyebrows?"

The balloon's pilot stepped out of the basket. He held a portable radio over his head and moved from place to place, searching for a signal.

Jack disentangled himself. There they were, acting like the whole thing was no big deal. "You did it again!" he shouted.

His mom dropped her arms. His dad stepped back.

"Yes, that's right," Jack said. "So don't act like we just got separated at the mall and now you've found me in the food court. You lost me in the Maasai Mara!"

"But we were chased by a bull," his mom said. "We couldn't have seen that coming . . ."

"That was a Cape buffalo, and of course you could have seen that coming!" Jack said. "You could have read the guidebook. You could have listened to the Maasai. They told you to turn back."

"He's right, Richard," his mom said, her face

reddening. "We did do it again. But, Jack, we tried so hard to follow your rules."

"We really felt we were following them to the letter," Jack's dad said.

"Guess what happened to me," Jack said, "I was stalked by hyenas and attacked by a honey badger." He reached into the backpack and pulled out the monkey. "Look what happened to him! This was a gift!"

Jack's mom and dad stared at the patched-up monkey.

"And you know what else?" he continued. "My eyebrows got burned off because you bought flammable sleeping bags. And that bull in musth the Maasai told us about is a deranged elephant that tried to knock down my tree. The tree I have been living in this whole time!"

Jack's mom looked over his shoulder. "Not that elephant, I hope," she said.

Jack turned. The bull elephant had paused at the top of the ridge. It looked in their direction and then thundered down the slope.

"Run!" Jack shouted.

His dad grabbed Jack's arm, and they raced

to the balloon. Jack flung himself over the side. His mom and dad jumped in after him. Jack scrambled to his feet as the balloon lifted off the ground. It rose quickly, floating thirty feet off the ground and rising higher by the second.

"Wait," Jack said, "where's that guy you came with?"

In which Jack drops in on Meticiki

Jack peered over the side. The pilot was still working on his radio, unaware that the balloon had taken off.

His mom leaned over the side and called down. "Captain Jenkins, we've a bit of a mishap on our hands. We'll have this sorted out directly."

"Directly," his dad echoed.

The pilot ran after the balloon. Jack leaned out of the basket, but he couldn't make out much of what the man was shouting. It sounded like "Kill you, something, knew it, something, bloody Berensons."

The balloon rose higher and higher. Jack realized that if they kept going, their new problem would be navigating a Mars landing. "Dad, how did you make it go up?"

"Simplest thing in the world, I just threw off the rope attached to the anchor and pulled a lever and up we went."

"Which lever?" Jack asked.

Jack's dad said, "Well, let's see. I was standing right here and I reached out . . . No, maybe I was standing just there, and I would have . . . "

Jack looked at the controls. There were two levers. A small flame burned overhead, heating the air inside the balloon. Jack slowly pulled on one of the levers. A flap opened at the top of the balloon. Hot air escaped with a whoosh, and the balloon began a rapid descent.

Jack pushed the lever the other way to close the flap and slow the balloon. The balloon continued to rush downward. If he didn't figure out how to make it go up again, they would crash. Jack pushed on the opposite lever. He heard a hissing sound above him, and the flame shot up. The balloon leveled out.

"Good show, Jack," his mom said. "Now we can just pop down and collect Jenkins."

Jack peeked over the side. Miles of plains, crowded with animals, and no sign of the pilot. "Where is he?"

His parents hung over the sides of the basket, scanning the landscape. "Now, that's unfortunate," his mom said.

"No worries, Claire," his dad said. "There—see? That's got to be the track we've flown over before. The village should be straight ahead."

"Good eye, Richard," his mom said. "We'll just fly over and tell them to be on the lookout for poor old Jenkins."

"What village?" Jack asked.

"Meticiki's," his dad said. "The first day we were out with Jenkins, we flew right over it. Since then, we've done a few flyovers to update Meticiki on our progress. He's extremely fond of us, you know."

Jack carefully pushed on one of the levers, slowly releasing some air from the balloon. Hopefully once they reached the village, they could hover at about twenty feet. After they had alerted Meticiki to go rescue the pilot, Jack could start thinking about how to land the balloon safely on the ground.

"Jack, you're a real natural at this," his mom said.

"I'm not planning a career as a balloon pilot, if that's what you're thinking," Jack said. "And I'm not going to forget you lost me again, if that's also what you're thinking. Have you been flying around in a balloon all this time? I sent up a smoke signal to flag one down."

"Good grief, Richard. That *was* a signal," his mom said.

"You were the one that said 'spontaneous combustion,'" his dad muttered.

The balloon drifted over the savannah. Below them, thousands of wildebeest trekked forward, sending up clouds of dust.

"Look," his mom cried. "There's the village, straight ahead! Now, we just want to fly low, right over it, and I'll send word about Jenkins. Then off we go for a champagne breakfast, easy as you please."

Jack pushed on the lever to release air. The

balloon picked up speed on descent. They were going way too fast. Jack fumbled with the controls.

Jack's dad said, "Let me help you with that, Son," and pushed the lever as far as it would go in the opposite direction. The flame died over Jack's head.

The balloon barreled toward the *enkang*. "Dad, you turned it the wrong way," Jack cried.

"Sorry," his dad yelled.

They crashed through the acacia fence, then hit the ground and rolled. Jack was thrown against the side of the basket. They finally came to a stop against the side of a building.

"Everybody all right?" Jack's mom asked, stumbling away from the basket. Jack crawled out with his dad behind him.

"Right as rain," his dad said, staggering to his feet. "Not as smooth a landing as old Jenkins would have pulled off, but I'd say it was pretty good for a first go."

"We weren't supposed to land at all," Jack said, examining a scrape on his elbow.

"Look," his mom said, "there's Meticiki."

A tall man in a red robe strode over to them.

Despite what his parents had said, Jack did not think the man looked extremely fond of them. Or at all fond of them. "Berenson," he said in a flat tone.

Jack's dad held his hand out to Meticiki and said, "You'll be relieved to know we found our little chap. Slight mishap with Jenkins, though."

Meticiki stood with his hands at his sides. Jack's dad dropped his outstretched hand and said, "Ah, I see you're a bit put out. We *did* come in a little hard. Guilty as charged."

"That," Meticiki said, pointing to the wrecked side of the building, "is my *manyatta*."

"Gosh, we're sorry," his mom said.

Meticiki glared at her. "The Berensons. They are always sorry."

"Sir," Jack said, "we'll fix the hole. We'll make your house good as new and then never bother you again."

Meticiki turned to Jack. "Where is Captain Jenkins?"

Jack gulped. "He's somewhere on the savannah. We accidentally left without him. Hopefully he's in a tree by now."

Meticiki folded his arms. “You have learned nothing from the Gradys?” he asked Jack’s parents. “It is not enough to leave two *wazungu* stranded? Now it is three?”

“Well, now,” Jack’s dad said, “it all happened rather fast. There we were, reuniting with Jack, and then there was an elephant heading our way, so we jumped into the balloon, and before we knew it . . . ”

A crowd had gathered behind Meticiki. A woman stepped forward and said, “What has happened to our house?”

“Berenson,” Meticiki said.

Whispers flew around Jack’s head. “Berenson? Berenson!”

The woman, who Jack assumed was Mrs. Meticiki, said, “We were promised they would never return.”

Meticiki pointed to Jack’s parents. “Get that balloon out of my village.” He turned to Jack and said, “Follow me.”

• • •

At the far end of the village, a young man

handed Meticiki a portable radio. Meticiki called the Mara Splendor Lodge and ended the transmission by saying, "Correct. The balloon is destroyed, Jenkins is on foot in the Mara, and they have demolished my house. It is the Berensons; how else could it have turned out?"

Meticiki motioned for Jack to sit down. Together, they leaned against an outbuilding, catching the shade from the roof. "Why are they here?" Meticiki asked.

"Oh," Jack said. "Well, they wanted to build a camp out here for tourists."

"What?"

"Didn't you get their letter? They wanted to hire you as a technical consultant. You know, someone to tell them how to do everything."

"I did not receive a letter," Meticiki said. "My brothers told me the Berensons looked for me. Since then, I have been asked many questions about the *wazungu* flying by in the balloon. I have been thinking about moving the village to a new piece of land."

"I wouldn't have blamed you," Jack said. "They're always sure that they're on the right track and everything will work out. And then it doesn't."

"Oh yes," Meticiki said, "always smiling and having a great time! No problem too big to make the Berensons sad. When the Gradys were missing, what did they say to me? 'No worries, Meticiki.' Two elderly *wazungu* missing somewhere in the bush, but I should not worry."

"I wrote family rules for them thinking it would make them less . . . accident-prone," Jack said.

"You cannot do it. You see this dog?" Meticiki said, pointing to a tan, medium-sized dog lying in the sun. "He does not look so different from the hyena. But you cannot bring a hyena into a village and expect he won't kill your cows."

Jack had to agree with that. But it wasn't really the hyena's fault that it would eat a cow. The hyena would just be doing what hyenas do.

Animals just followed their instincts.

Maybe that was the problem. Maybe his parents didn't have instincts.

"When will you go to live with others your age?" Meticiki asked. "You will be safer there."

"I'll live with my parents until I'm eighteen."

"That is many years. How will you survive?"

"I don't know," Jack said. "But I better think of something."

...

The men of the village had dragged the wrecked balloon out of the *enkang*. Jack's parents were patching the hole in Meticiki's house under the baleful eye of Mrs. Meticiki.

"Hey there, Son," his dad said, smoothing brown material over a pattern of sticks. "Here we are building an *inkajijik*, exactly like we planned. Just not our *inkajijik*. Good practice though . . . "

Jack's mom passed mud and cow dung to his dad and said, "Luv, we know things went . . . slightly off course. But your father and I have talked about it, and we're determined that nothing like this will ever happen again. Ever."

"Not even one more time," his dad said.

"Really," Jack said. "And how are you going to make sure?"

"What we will do is—" his dad said, "Well,

for one thing, no more driving near bulls in musth. I don't care if they're regular bulls or bull elephants or bull buffalos. We won't even go near a bulldog."

"No more bulls," his mom added. "Never again, and that is final."

"You don't get it," Jack said. "You don't see the real problem. You don't use good instincts. If you have them in you somewhere, they haven't come out. So you just go around acting like wild hyenas or something."

"We've been called worse . . ." his mom mumbled.

"This problem has got to be fixed," Jack said. "I want to live long enough to go to college. If we don't do something about it, what happens next? You leave me at the top of Mount Kilimanjaro because you thought I was right behind you? I suppose I'm lucky the *Titanic* isn't around anymore. I'm sure we would have been the first family to get on the ship."

"Kilimanjaro? The *Titanic*?" his mom said. "We would never—"

"Not in a million years," his dad said.

"Are you sure?" Jack asked.

"Pretty sure," his mom said quietly.

"Finish repairing Meticiki's house," Jack said sternly. "Then we'll go to the lodge to pay for that balloon and make sure Captain Jenkins is safe. Then we are going to the coast."

"The beach!" his mom said. "That's brilliant. I was sure you'd insist on going straight home to Pennsylvania."

"Don't get your hopes up," Jack said. "There will be no opportunities to accidentally harpoon me with a speargun or forget me at a dive site or fling me off the back of a Jet Ski. We're going to Namaste For Kids. It's a resort for families. We'll do yoga and make pottery. And that's all."

His mom and dad looked at each other. His dad said, "Well, I suppose a person never can have too many pots."

"While I'm recovering by the pool," Jack continued, "I'll examine the adults at the resort. I'll point out the really outstanding examples of parents with good instincts so you can follow them around and study them. Hopefully, that will help your own parent instincts come out."

He sighed and said quietly, "I'm hoping they're just lying dormant somewhere."

"We'll do exactly what you say, Jack," his mom said.

"We'll find those parent instincts if it kills us," his dad said.

Meticiki put his hand on Jack's shoulder. "You face the Berensons with courage."

Jack's face flushed with pride. He had not expected a warrior like Meticiki to think he was courageous.

"Look at you, rascal," his mom said. "Hanging around with the chief."

"That's our boy," his dad said.

Meticiki stared at Jack's parents. He turned to Jack and handed him a smooth, foot-long wooden club. "Take my *orinka*. Courage may not be enough."

Jack took the gift from Meticiki. "Thank you. I'm sure I won't have to use it. After all, I really don't see how my mom and dad could get in trouble doing yoga and making pots."

Meticiki did not look convinced.

About the Author

Lisa Doan received a master's degree in writing for children and young adults from Vermont College of Fine Arts. As a professional vagabond, she has traveled extensively through Africa and Asia and lived on a Caribbean island for eight years. Her variety of occupations has included master scuba diving instructor, New York City headhunter, owner-chef of a Chinese restaurant, television show set medic, and deputy prothonotary of a county court. She wrote her first book during a Caribbean slow season while waiting for restaurant customers. She currently lives in Pennsylvania with a Great Dane who stares her down for biscuits.

About the Illustrator

Ivica Stevanovic has illustrated picture books such as *The Royal Treasure Measure* and *Monsters Can Mosey*, as well as book covers and graphic novels. He also teaches classes at the Academy of Art in Novi Sad, in northern Serbia. He lives in Veternik, northern Serbia, with his wife, Milica, who is also a children's illustrator, and their daughter, Katarina.

VIA AIR MAIL